I Have a Garden

I Have a Garden

Bob Barner

Holiday House / New York

For Cathie and Jean. Two great gardeners.

I LIKE TO READ is a registered trademark of Holiday House, Inc.

Copyright © 2013 by Bob Barner
All Rights Reserved
HOLIDAY HOUSE is registered in the U.S. Patent and Trademark Office.
Printed and Bound in November 2013 at Tien Wah Press, Johor Bahru, Johor, Malaysia.
The artwork was made with paper collage, gouache, pastel, and pencil.
www.holidayhouse.com
3 5 7 9 10 8 6 4 2
Library of Congress Cataloging-in-Publication Data
Barner, Bob.
I have a garden / Bob Barner. — 1st ed.
p. cm. — (I like to read)
Summary: Relates the wonderful things that can be found in a garden.
ISBN 978-0-8234-2527-3 (hardcover)
[1. Gardens—Fiction.] I. Title.
PZ7.B2597Iam 2013
[E]—dc23
2011041293

ISBN 978-0-8234-3056-7 (paperback)
GRL B

I have a garden.

I have a frog in my garden.

I have a bird in my garden.

I have a chipmunk
in my garden.

I have a bug in my garden.

I have a bee.

I have a butterfly.

I have a snail.

And I have many flowers.

This garden is all for me.

No. This garden is
for all of us.

We have a garden.

I Like to Read® Books in Paperback
You will like all of them!

Visit http://www.holidayhouse.com/I-Like-to-Read/
for more about I Like to Read® books, including
flash cards, reproducibles, and the complete list of titles.